Other Ashridge Bears books you will enjoy

Ashridge Christmas
Birthday Surprise
Fun on the Pond
Visitors to Stay
Winter's Coming

Text © Margaret Carter 1993
Illustrations © Richard Fowler 1993
First published 1993 by
Campbell Books
This edition published 1995 by
Campbell Books
12 Half Moon Court · London EC1A 7HE
Printed in Great Britain by Cambus Litho Ltd

ISBN 1 85292 254 0 (paperback)

The Birthday Surprise

Margaret Carter
Richard Fowler

CAMPBELL BOOKS

– and in the middle of the wood, was a small house.

A very special day

There was once a great wood called Ashridge which grew on the sides of steep hills overlooking peaceful countryside.

Many creatures lived in the wood – foxes, deer, badgers, squirrels, hedgehogs – and in the middle of the wood, so carefully hidden that no one would ever find it unless they had a map, was a small house.

And in this house lived a family of bears.

In the family was a father, a mother and three children – Tim, George and Daisy.

Tim was the eldest – he was rather quiet. George was in the middle – he wasn't at all quiet. Daisy, the baby, was sometimes very quiet and sometimes very noisy.

The Bear family had many friends among the creatures of the wood. They all lived very happily together and each day there was something different to do.

One morning as soon as George woke up he
remembered it was a very special day. 'Tim, Tim!'
he called to his brother in the other bed, 'wake up!
It's mother's birthday and we've got to get her
surprise ready!'

'I am awake,' said Tim's voice from beneath
the bedclothes. 'I've been awake for hours!
I've been waiting for you! Now come on, get up
quickly. We've promised to lay the breakfast.
Don't make a sound – we mustn't wake them.'

They crept out of the bedroom, then,
'Listen!' said George.

Thump, thump, plop, thump!

'Daisy's awake,' said Tim, with a sigh.
'That's her throwing things out of her
cot. We'd better take her downstairs.'

Daisy was very glad to see them as
she'd grown tired of throwing toys about
and was feeling the need for company.

'Daisy,' said George, lifting her out
of the cot, 'you must be very *very* quiet.'

'Ssh, ssh, ssh,' agreed Daisy.

They tiptoed downstairs. Daisy crawled down backwards on her knees because she was young and her legs were still wobbly.

'Now,' said Tim, when they were in the kitchen, 'let's begin. What do we need? Bowls and spoons.' 'Plates and knives,' said George, 'and cups and saucers for the grown-ups.'

'Mugs for us and Daisy's cup for Daisy. Now for the honey, bread and milk,' said Tim, putting them on the table.

Was there anything else? 'Yes,' said George and he fetched the cornflakes.

They put birthday cards in Mother Bear's place and decorated her chair with streamers. The table looked lovely except that George thought they needed flowers.

He picked some from the garden and put them in a vase, then he climbed on a stool to reach the centre of the table.

'That's funny,' he said, staring. 'Where's the honey gone?'

At that moment the stool tipped over and George sat down suddenly on the floor. Now he could see under the table and under the table was Daisy – a very sticky Daisy – eating the honey! 'That will not *do*, Daisy!' he said. Then, *crunch!* He was walking on cornflakes! Daisy had spilt them all over the floor. 'Kiss, kiss,' she said to show she was sorry but, 'No thanks!' said George, 'you're too sticky to kiss!'

'Quick, quick, they're coming,' cried Tim.

'*That's funny*,' *he said, staring. '*Where's the honey gone?*'*

They only just had time to sweep the
cornflakes under the table and give Daisy's
face a quick wipe (which she did not like)
before Mother Bear came into the room.

'Why, you've laid the table,' she said,
'and what lovely cards! Oh thank you,
children.' So father warmed the milk and
made the tea, then they all had breakfast.
(But mother didn't know – yet – what a
terrible mess there was under the table.)

The secret

The bears were just finishing breakfast when they heard a tap at the front door.

It was a blackbird with a message. 'Mrs. Fox invites Mother Bear to lunch,' he said.

'Well, that would be nice,' said mother, 'but I really don't know . . .'

'Nonsense, my dear,' said father, 'go and enjoy yourself.'

'If you insist,' said mother. She put on her hat and they all waved her goodbye.

As soon as she had gone, the bears (and
Blackbird) did a little dance of triumph.
Their plan had worked! With mother away they
could now prepare her surprise.

'Put on your hats and aprons,' said father,
'and wash your hands while I get out
everything we need for cooking.'

They did this very quickly, then they
began. Father rolled the pastry, Tim cut the
shapes, George filled, Daisy watched. Jam tarts,
strawberry tarts, apple tarts, sausage rolls,
ham rolls – then suddenly, 'Cooe!' Mother
Bear had *come back*!

Whatever could they do? In one moment she would be in the kitchen and see the surprise! Then, 'I've come back to pick some flowers for Mrs. Fox,' she called.

'I'll help,' called George, running into the garden. 'Bring wrapping paper, Tim!'

Father waited anxiously. Daisy's eyes were round as saucers. Then, 'Thank you, boys,' they heard mother say and off she went once more.

She had never once seen into the kitchen!

Father gave a big sigh of relief. 'Well done, boys,' he said. 'Well done!'

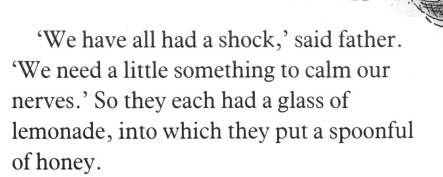

'We have all had a shock,' said father.
'We need a little something to calm our
nerves.' So they each had a glass of
lemonade, into which they put a spoonful
of honey.

Then, 'Dad, dad, dad!' shrieked Daisy,
waving her spoon about in an agitated
manner. Smoke was coming from the oven!

They had forgotten the sausage rolls!

Fortunately these were not black, but just a rather dark brown. They ate them at once and found them delicious – not tasting brown at all.

Then once again they stirred and mixed – sponge cakes, honey cakes, fruit cakes, until every shelf in the larder was full.

Except the top shelf.

'It is time,' said father, 'to make the birthday cake.'

They all shivered with excitement.

And there was the cake. Looking divine, smelling delicious.

Flour and sugar, milk and eggs, one by one they were brought to the table and tipped into the big yellow bowl. 'Father,' cried George, 'the bowl's too small!' Indeed, the bowl was already full and there were fruit and cherries still to go in.

So they turned it all into a bigger bowl and carried on stirring. When everything was well mixed they plopped it into a tin and slid it into the oven.

Then they sat and waited.

It was an anxious time.

At last, *ping!* 'Time's up,' said Tim. And there was the cake. Looking divine, smelling delicious.

'Yum, yum,' said Daisy.

'Now we must put the marzipan on,' said father, 'and the icing and the candles. Then it will be ready.'

Very carefully he smoothed marzipan and then icing all over the cake. Daisy was allowed to put cherries round the edges. The boys put candles in the middle – 'Just a few will do,' said father.

It was ready. They put it on the top shelf of the larder and locked the door.

Then they all washed up together, after which they had a snack – biscuits and milk so as not to spoil their appetites.

Now all they had to do was wait for mother to come back.

Happy birthday, Mother Bear

When mother came back from seeing Mrs. Fox
Daisy was fast asleep, lopsided, in her
high chair.

'Has she been good?' asked mother because –
being a baby – Daisy sometimes needed a great
deal of attention.

'Very good,' said father. 'No trouble at
all,' said Tim.

Just then Daisy woke up. She smiled at mother then pointed to the larder. 'Cake,' she said.

'She wants something to eat,' said mother going towards the larder.

'Oh no,' called father. 'She can't be hungry. She's had lots to eat, hasn't she, boys?'

'Masses,' said Tim. 'Oodles,' said George.

But still Daisy shouted, 'cake, cake, cake!'

'Whatever can she mean?' wondered mother. 'She seems to be trying to tell me something!'

'Perhaps she wants a drink,' said George.

'And she's got the words muddled,' said Tim.

'Here you are, Daisy,' said George, 'have a drink.' He knew, you see, if Daisy drank she couldn't talk.

'I stayed longer than I meant to with Mrs. Fox,' said mother. 'Now I'll just take my hat upstairs, then we'll all have supper.'

'No need to hurry,' said father. When mother had gone upstairs he turned to the boys. 'I can't stand any more shocks,' he said. 'First mother nearly came back, then the sausage rolls got burnt, now Daisy's saying, 'cake . . .' '

'Cheer up, father, it's nearly time,' said George. He looked out of the window then called to his brother. 'Come and see, Tim.'

'Yes,' said Tim, smiling. 'They're all here!'

'Now my dears,' said mother, coming into
the room, 'tell me what you've been doing
today.'

'Nothing much,' said Tim.

'This and that,' said George.

'Cake, ca . . .' began Daisy but George coughed
very loudly, so mother didn't hear.

'It's such a lovely evening,' said father,
with a wink at the boys, 'I thought we could
have supper outside.' And he opened the
front door of the cottage.

And there was the surprise! All the creatures
of the wood had come to mother's party.

Foxes with their cubs, deer peeping from
behind flowers, rabbits sitting tall to
watch, and in the centre stood Badger
who now raised one paw for silence.
Then down it came and with one voice all
the company sang, 'Happy Birthday, Mother
Bear, Happy Birthday to you.'

Mother Bear was quite overcome.

'Oh my dears,' she cried, 'what a surprise! But have we enough food for all our guests?'

'Look,' said Tim.

Out of the house they came. Mice and rats, hares and rabbits, hedgehogs and moles – all carrying trays of food.

'We made all the food,' said the children.

'I brought the message,' sang the blackbird.

'And I,' said Mrs. Fox with a slow, secret smile, 'kept you talking!'

The sun grew lower in the sky. Shadows crept across the grass. The light from the cottage doorway made a yellow path along which was brought yet more food and drink.

Until once more Badger called for silence.

Crickets sang like a roll of tiny drums and along the path came Tim, George and Daisy, carrying the cake.

Out of the house they came.

'Magnificent,' said Badger and there were tears in his eyes, although usually he was a serious sort of person.

Mother blew out the candles. The children handed round slices – everyone agreed it was quite delicious. Quite.

And after the eating, came the dancing. Father led out his wife in a graceful waltz accompanied by a chorus of nightingales, specially hired for the party.

Four rabbits danced a reel, Squirrel
gave a short but spirited display of
leaping, Hare danced a hornpipe on a
tree stump and Fox and his wife performed
a most exciting tango.

Blackbirds whistled, owls hooted, bats
fluttered and Mole turned head over heels
so often he grew dizzy and had to be
fanned with a dock leaf.

The moon looked down and seemed to
smile, the stars shone, then slowly, slowly
the singing grew quieter. Badger gave
the most enormous yawn. Owl dozed a little
and nearly fell off his branch. Mole
disappeared into his tunnel.

It was time to end the party.

One by one they thanked their hosts and
crept silently away into the shadows.

Once again the forest was quiet and only
the trees rustled gently in the night breeze.
In the distance Mrs. Fox called to the last
of her children to come home.

In the darkness a hedgehog snored and a
ladybird giggled.

But where were the children?

They found them under the table, fast asleep and so tired they didn't wake even when they were carried up to their beds and carefully tucked in.

Then father and mother crept away to their own bed. 'I have never, ever, had such a wonderful . . .' but mother didn't finish the word, 'birthday' – she was asleep. And even if she had, why – father wouldn't have heard since he too was fast asleep.

And out in the wood everyone else was also asleep – except the night creatures who are meant to stay awake.

And even they looked rather tired.